Familial Phantasmagorial

Spike Brown

Illustrated by

Karl Whiteley

Tower Bridge Books

Copyright © Spike Brown 2024

ISBN: 978-1-80558-186-4

A catalogue record of this book is available from the British Library

Contents

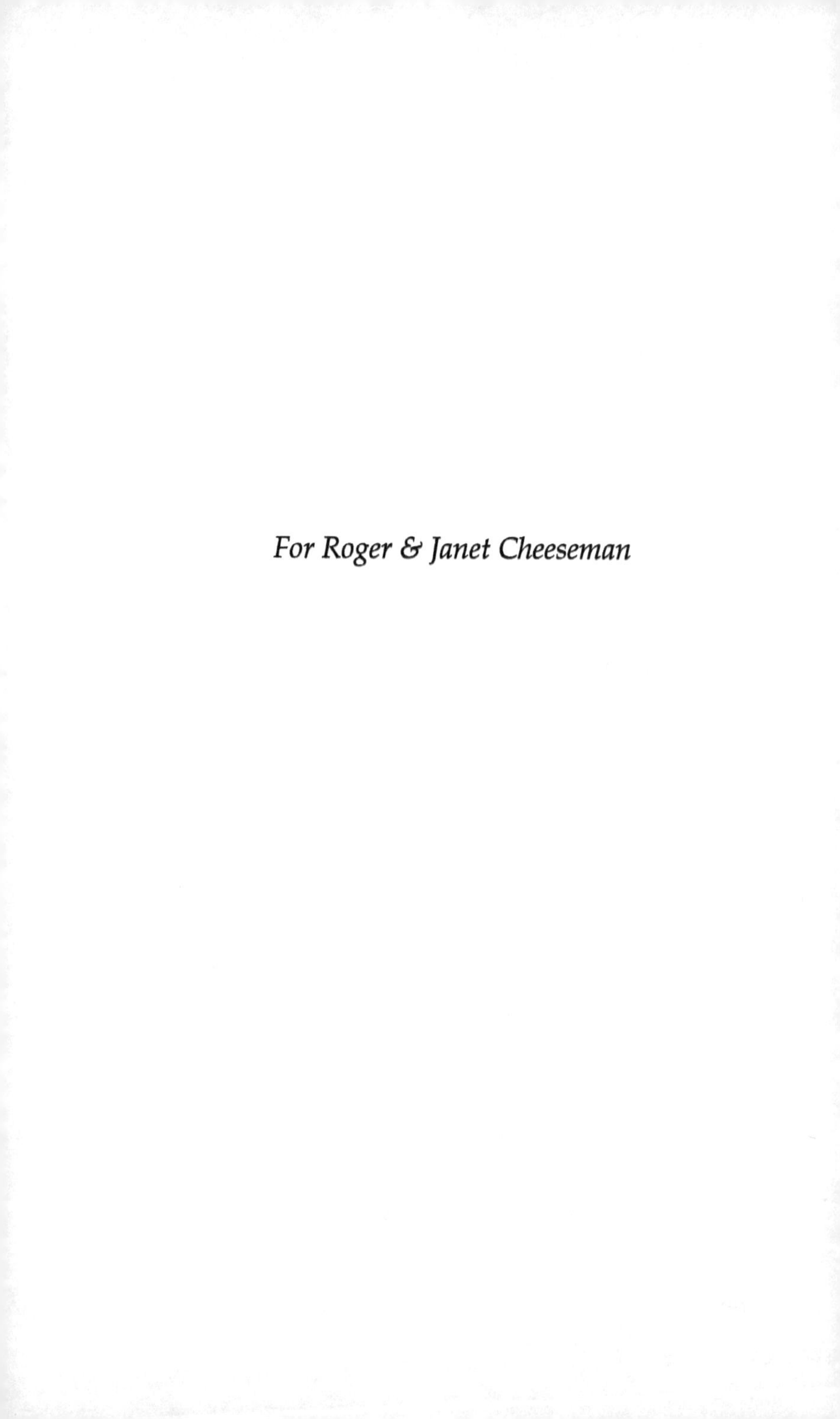

For Roger & Janet Cheeseman

LOCAL LIBRARY

My niece and I by way of Little Thornden station, had ventured to town by train and were at the main library, where my friend Mr Newbold, who looked after rare books and manuscripts, was at pains to offer us every civility.

"I'm glad you found my niece's journals fairly challenging, at least, were interested enough to study the content concerning blood cultists in fairy tale literature."

"Your niece's work was commendable, a starting point it so happens, for what I have long been wishing to draw to your attention, as a PSYCHICAL INVESTIGATOR."

Emboldened by praise for her literary efforts, Ligea only wished for further accolades, for all attention to be focused on her – thus by means of a stern admonishing glance, I urged her to desist, "pray, continue Freddie – we are all ears."

Pouring us each a cup of tea from the pot upon his desk, the librarian nodded. "Mr Lensby, may I draw your attention to the ship's log of Captain C.E. Johns. An eyewitness report from the year 1886." Choosing a digestive biscuit, I settled back into my chair.

"Captain Johns commands the whaler S.S. Theron, a 575-ton steam vessel plying the ice floes off Greenland up in the Arctic Circle. During a gale the ship broke away from the rest of the pack. The crew were never idle, employed by hunting seals and sea elephants, clubbing them to death on the ice. A bloody, visceral business, but nothing so bloody as capturing, that is harpooning, whales surfacing on the frozen sea, thence skinning them for blubber, which is the main purpose of such a perilous voyage north. For this season, however, whales proved elusive. The crew disheartened for the processing of whales meant much hard work, but of course considerably increased income."

"According to this witness report, the whaling vessel had run up through crowded brash, forcing plates of ice many yards long beneath the keel and came, for a time, to be lodged in the pack ice. Thus, men on deck brandishing axes took the opportunity to hack away ice encrusted to the ship's side and rigging. A normal occupational hazard at this northerly latitude. At 5pm, upon the 24th of February, from out of the frost smoke, was spied from the wheelhouse a three-masted vessel under sail in a southwest wind. Flags fluttering from its masts bore not the usual ensigns, designs of nations, but instead trailing weepers more consistent to a funeral barge in Venice. I shall quote directly from the log:

Superstitious fancies aside. Despite concerns

for the ship's morbid aspect, we saw a boat hoisted

out and showing obvious camaraderie – one sea-

going vessel to another, a very jolly tourist party, a

group of chattering ladies supported by sailors

expertly handling the oars and tiller, rowing across

the shining sound between ice floes towards us.

Utilising most skilfully the channels of clear water

to reach our anchorage. I, along with my fellow

officers, having gathered upon the prow to welcome

aboard our visitors. At this juncture, I can report I

saw no reason for caution, nor indeed felt any

apprehension.

The long boat was well within a bowshot when

the tallest of the women, a truly beautiful lady of

noble bearing who wore a beaver-skin hat, white

fur cloak and long jewel-encrusted, high-collared

gown of some rich velvet material stood up.

Thereafter indicating to various baskets

stowed in the rowing boat, called out:

"Will you allow I, Countess Vashtek of Prague, to board your ship, Captain? To join me in a modest banquet, my equerries and handmaidens, your officers and crew besides?" The countess possessed such an infectious spirit of gaiety I confess I never thought to question for one instant what such a group of ladies, whom I presumed to be wealthy aristocratic personages, should be doing this far north in the first place.

The inconsistencies did not enter my mind. "I bring eatables of gelinottes, coqs de Bruyéres, crawfish as large as lobsters, pheasants from

Bohemia, boar, plenty of fish and fowl, green peas,

artichokes, asparagus – enough to satisfy any

amongst you who be gourmands."

"Your offer is too kind, ma'am. I and my crew

should be honoured. You have found your sea legs

at any rate, Countess of Prague. Well, well, I have

never visited that great city of a hundred spires."

"Oh, I am from Hradčany, the seat of Czech

Royalty. I frequent the castle, I am a close relation

of Prince Rupert, you see, although Captain, let us

be frank, I myself perceive it matters little what lofty

station in life one occupies. For out here in this

desolate continent of ice and snow Mother Nature rules supreme. Being the greatest of levellers."

"How can anyone argue with such wisdom, Countess?" I agreed, beginning to supervise my crew's careful, always attentive transferral of the group of waiting figures, the boat's delightful company, across the ice, up the steps to our gang plank.

Once on board, the Countess of Prague's aides charmingly distributed wicker baskets full of plentiful victuals to members of my besotted, disbelieving crew.

I, the shipmaster, a normally dour and taciturn man, uneasy in female company, found myself kissing that fair noblewoman's hand, pompously leading the countess, accompanied by her maidservant, Anna Basek, across the deck as though to the strains of Mendelsohn's triumphal Wedding March.

The captain's quarters were tidy and acceptable. I thus ordered the table to be laid with the finest cutlery, tableware and starched linen we could provide. I invited my Norwegian first officer, Carlsen, a ladies' man and assured conversationalist, to sit in on the sumptuous dinner.

However, part way during the meal certain worrying issues arose and begging the ladies leave to superintend my men, I and my first officer hastily retired to the wheelhouse, where we might not be overheard. My chief engineer on watch broke into our hushed conversation with the following astounding intelligence:

"The sailors crewing that black ship in yonder sound, the three-masted vessel?"

"Aye, what of them?"

"Through the wheelhouse window, using my telescope earlier. I perceived t'is not men on board, moving about the deck performing shipboard tasks, Captain Johns, but rather knobbly-jointed, life-sized puppets, marionettes busy as ants. What are we to make of such devilry — is your countess the puppet master to her subservient crew of woodentops, that Vashtec woman you invited on board?"

"Witch work!" exclaimed my first officer emphatically.

"We are, I fear, Captain, nestling under a pall

of evil magic."

"I concur," said I, realising every one of us on board was in dire peril. "Cram, Jock Cram — where is my irascible Scotsman?"

"Below decks, sir," answered my chief engineer, one of the most level-headed practical men I knew. "Sleeping off his grog, a-lying in his bunk."

"Then for heaven's sake wake him. Fetch him to me. We have but little time to formulate a plan — and the ship's surgeon. Be quick about it!"

It turned out, oblivious to on-board festivities,

the doctor was studying his learned books in his cabin.

"Fetch Jock Cram," I repeated.

Thus, it was, with profuse apologies to the Countess of Prague, managing, along with my first officer, to keep up an entire pretence of casual affability, we re-joined our female guests.

"I trust, ma'am, your broth is to your liking. You seem barely to have touched your meal."

"Oh, my captain, that does not detract from my joy at being in ship's company once more. Although I presently hunger for a more sustaining liquor, a warm Burgundy wine. Alas, I have little appetite for victuals."

I thus jovially tucked into my Bohemian pheasant with gusto, for, as pre-arranged, it was to be my brave Norwegian first officer whom I left to make the initial move. To begin in earnest to confront the forces of darkness, draw them into battle on-board ship before we ourselves limply fell victim to this unholy alliance.

Using all the male charm Carlsen could muster, albeit somewhat overfamiliar, he purred:

"Might I pass you, dearest Anna, some more of

this delicious cloudberry sauce. My sweet lady, you just have no idea how wondrous is this feast provided by your esteemed mistress for us whalers, out here in the Arctic for many months at a time."

Thus, the maidservant, shyly stretching out her hand, smiling coquettishly to receive the proffered jug, suspected nothing. Carlsen, meanwhile, seized his opportunity well, fiercely raking the prongs of his dinner fork across the top of her delicate hand. Unbelievably, supple moist clay emanated from the furrowed wound.

"You, a golem!" My first officer's voice sounded

derisive; he remained single-minded and fearless.

"Did your mistress fashion you and the others upon the night of a full moon, model you in female guise from a wheelbarrow load of heavy, sticky, graveyard clay? An infernal potter, indeed!"

Carlsen, like myself, fascinated that we should have a golem in our midst, in a thrice scraped his pronged fork, this time upward along Anna Basek's exposed wrist, renting forth the synthetic flesh, prompting still more brick-red clay to ooze from the gash, dirtying the pristine tablecloth.

The spell was broken; the maidservant

screaming, incensed by her undoing, changed instantly into a bland 'chocolate box' clay image of herself yet to be properly fired in a kiln, although it must be recorded her wide, thumb-smoothed mouth was crammed with horribly razor-sharp teeth.

If this incident were not enough, determined to do my part, I boldly thrust a crucifix in the face of the beautiful Countess Vashtek, a centuries old vampire of long standing I had no doubt.

"Make swift your return to the fiery furnaces of hell, madam," I pronounced with all the gravity

beholden to a Methodist preacher, expecting instant destruction. But, flashing her deadly fangs, she appeared not unduly troubled, merely mischievously causing certain items of tableware to rise into the air and fly about my cabin.

Whilst wine glasses and plates levitated, crashing into one another, showering us with debris, during the ensuing commotion the golem and its mistress, whatever her fabulous looks, none better than a base, predatory creature, jumped up from their chairs and made a run for the cabin door. The countess, desperate to win the freedom of the deck to assert her will, for she was thirsty for the

blood of I and my crewmates, whom I expected she

deemed little better than a herd of wintering cattle.

However, I was having none of that.

Unbeknown to the countess, one of my

collaborators, old Jock Cram, lay in wait, biding his

time up at the prow Manning the harpoon gun

upon its swivel base. No sooner did the canny

Scotsman perceive her, even before she could react,

than a lethal harpoon, along with a trailing rope,

shot and aimed faultlessly, sallied through the air

striking the vampire through the heart, pinning

her to the timber planking of the wheelhouse.

As prearranged, the ship's doctor, Clancy, rushed forward and swiftly lopped off her gorgeous head with an axe. Stowing it, despite orders otherwise, into his leather Gladstone bag for future scientific study.

The golem, Anna, along with the fleeing equerries alike fashioned in clay beneath their dazzling baroque exterior, we dealt with by means of nets and ice axes. Once despatched, flinging them overboard, a thick residue of wet clay staining the ice floes brick red for some while afterward. We watched as, against all logical reasoning to any

God-fearing Christian, the vessel burst into flame,

thence dozens of clattering, clacking marionettes

catching fire on deck, performing a twitching

dance of death more entertaining than any theatre

troupe of toy soldiers. The puppets' hinged jaws

studded with sharp nails for teeth, noisily

clamping and unclamping, every wooden joint

screeching as they were immolated to nought but

ash, burnt to hellish cinders along with that

sinister vessel - beneath the decks of which I was

later informed resided a revolting ossuary. A

repository for the skeletal remains of certain

former human prey, gnawed clean by the flesh-

loving, nail-teethed wooden marionettes and the

equally voracious golem."

The librarian replaced the somewhat worn logbook with the frayed leather binding back on his imposing desk, lifted the lid of the teapot and gave a cursory glance inside.

"And this really happened?" My niece enquired, returning her own empty cup to the tray. "I think it's a fraud, awfully well written though."

"Documented and verified by experts. The county records should never keep this under file otherwise. Point of fact, Mr Lensby, Dr Clancy the ship's surgeon who is mentioned in this account, practiced for many years in Eastlea. He personally swore to the encounter. I have written affidavits to that effect, but there's more. Hup, hup, let's hurry downstairs to storage."

That afternoon was to be a whirlwind of impressions, beginning with this trip to the basement, situated beneath the library's main portico and staircase hall.

We found ourselves in a large room dedicated to the storage of books which, often as not, I presumed were displayed in the galleries on a rotational basis.

We were led confidentially across to a section of blank wall.

Deftly activating a foot pedal just behind an open trunk containing more volumes; a panel swished upwards pistoned by compressed air, revealing that which was cleverly concealed in the secret hiding place. A handsome teak, glass-fronted display cabinet inlaid with green baize material.

Curious to view its contents, I instinctively shuddered, for staring back was a pristine human skull. Most notable, the relic possessed along its row of upper teeth a pair of ferocious fangs.

"Grandpapa the fangs are awfully sharp aren't they," said Legia. "A student's prank, perhaps?"

"This skull belongs to none other than Countess Vashtec of Prague. Her decapitated head, you will recall, bagged up by Dr Clancy shortly after she had been harpooned."

"He brought it back to this country aboard the whaler," my niece surmised.

"Just so young lady, to Thurso, the Theron's home port at the northernmost tip of Scotland. The medical notes state that any facial tissue and abundant hair quickly vanished, her beautiful features eradicated, dissolved by carbons in the air, but no putrefaction took place, as such, no bacterium to speak of."

"And both the upper and lower quadrants remain intact. Including her delicate barbed fangs resembling an angler's fishing fly hooks."

"Done, and it is this unique skull, the Countess of Prague's, which in a jiffy I intend to purloin and convey forthwith across the room to that desk. "

The desk I might say was furbished with a little porcelain sink, a clutter of pipettes, Bunsen burner, bottles, and glass tubes.

"The skull," Mr Newbold started the demonstration, "I have, you see, placed inside this cube, a vacuum- sealed glass tank. By utilising my apparatus, a mix of chemical crystals reacting together, I intend to force, to induce temperatures of below freezing... You will now notice that frost smoke is already forming inside the glass, fronds of ice crystallising around the casing of the cube. But have either of you considered the skull itself? What are your observations young lady?"

"The skull is becoming coated by a wafer-thin layer of ice," Ligea Barclay remarked, "the fangs appear more extracted, drawing out."

Following this interaction, the librarian bid us come

closer.

The next few minutes I categorise as being quite astounding.

A rapid transformation of matter was beginning to be generated.

The colder the tank got, even allowing for the misty glass, the more a human face, a pretty one at that, gradually emerged, encasing the bare skull. Blonde hair, both thick and plaited, grew abundantly completely recovering once again, the original personality. Creating a most attractive head that sapped all my attention.

The sheer beauty...

We were witness to newly materialised blue eyes peering inquisitively about them, twitching nostrils, the beginnings of a charming full-lipped, voluptuous smile.

I felt myself becoming more and more entranced, captivated, stimulated by such beauty.

"I shall cease the experiment now!" the librarian called out. The demonstration was at an end.

Mr Newbold twisted the cap to allow hot steam to rise in the cube. Thus, as swiftly the Countess of Prague's facial features blossomed into life and vitality, all too soon reduced to a bone yard relic, a chalky white skull bearing fangs, empty eye sockets staring blankly ahead from the glass cube.

Freddie Newbold back in his office was at his desk, part bathed in firelight, nursing a cup of tea, staring thoughtfully at the leather-bound ship's log placed neatly atop of a pile of my niece's exercise books tied up in rubber bands.

"Jolly clever — but how did you attain such knowledge?" Asked Ligea.

"Fleshing out the face, you mean, triggering the skull's ability to regenerate? Why, from Dr Clancy's detailed medical notes. For upon his death, a long-time resident of the town the Countess of Prague's skull, together with old apparatus, the log, provenance, and a box-file, were donated to the main library. You will conjecture he had himself dallied with forcing a low temperature in a container. I must hasten to add, strictly for research purposes and, like us today, very careful to allow the countess to rejuvenate her own head but briefly. I should emphasise, Milton, we rarely, if ever, tamper with that skull. I naturally trust you to remain tight-lipped about all that concerned us this afternoon, especially the concealed cabinet."

"Of course," I answered emphatically. "We have enjoyed this afternoon's foray immensely."

ARTHUR GETS A THICK EAR

One morning during the winter, found me ensconced in my study, a cheery fire crackling in the grate — I was chatting with my friend Mr Jopson, he, who had written a large number of books (mostly on black magic, else philosophical reflections) and so doing, become quite wealthy.

"*De nugis curialium*, by Walter Map — you have read it?" I enquired, choosing my favourite tobacco pipe from the spinning rack. "Medieval writer. First class stories about ghosts, goblins, and wood nymphs. Ligea my niece recommends him highly."

A knock at the door announced my housekeeper. Mrs Norton looked ashen, most perplexed.

"An odd circumstance, a terribly bad circumstance – that young lady we talked of. I beg you Mr Lensby, come at once. To Arthur's quarters."

I must emphasise – Arthur and Tubby my Grandsons, were during weekdays then involved in the science and practice of farming at the agricultural college – and my house in the village of Little Thornden was nicely placed, for they were easily able to cycle into Benbridge Stow, where the rural institute was situated. I'd always regarded Tubby more of a romantic lead, susceptible to a pretty face, an effortless charmer, very easy going with the fairer sex – Arthur, I'd normally felt was a bit slow, needed prompting – a game of darts, a few beers inside him to open up - We achieved the upstairs landing briskly.

I read out loud from a card. "Young gentlemen may at weekends entertain lady friends in their rooms between the hours of 1pm and 6pm – provided they have signed the book. You know the rules Arthur, where is she, this, I quote, 'fabulously attractive young lady in a white flowing gown?' You were seen with her last evening – speak up, sir, and soundly, for your continued stay at my house depends upon it."

My grandson remained tight lipped, wholly

unresponsive. "Come now, my housekeeper was forced to knock you up early and conclude this matter we surely shall."

Somewhat reluctantly, Arthur indicated to the 'slept in' bed whereon lay a sheeted lump.

"Did you do her a violence, kill her? By heavens, if you have it's the police for you, my boy," I directed sternly. Thankfully, I saw no blood nor signs of a struggle — the guest rooms appeared neat and tidy.

At last, Arthur found courage. "Grandfather, I swear to you, as a gentleman and a farming student of principle and considerable enterprise, I did indeed entertain a young woman of both grace and charm to tea and muffins in my room. Beyond this, my memory is but hazy. I, alas, recall little of the encounter, save her great beauty."

"She blasted well lies in your bed!" I exclaimed, rightly incensed. "Besides where you yourself sleep, simply admit it."

"Not she," he cried bitterly. "No, not she."

"For goodness sake Arthur," said I, "Enough of this affected twaddle, draw back the bed sheet and let us have done. The lady must be in here somewhere, why not your bed? Mrs Norton is aware of all the comings and goings and reports as such."

My grandson's nerves were in tatters. Needing

little further prompting, the young man finally acquiesced.

"GOOD GOD, what is that... *that thing?*" Mr Jopson seized my arm, a look of horror writ large upon his walrus-moustached, genial features, joining me in an audible gasp.

For beheld in our midst was some strange palpitating creature.

Leathery, veiny wings were folded in upon itself, the hairy snout and beseeching eyes bore some semblance to a giant rat species with antennae, yet the body undoubtedly taken the form of a monstrous grasshopper. The multiple legs twitched spasmodically; a greenish secretion ran freely from its nose stub. Arthur rushed to the sink and vomited profusely. I confess, my own stomach heaved uncomfortably, but I bore down the rising bile, approaching the bed as best I could.

"What are you?" I demanded to know.

"Amelia Lang," came a timid feminine response. I took in every part of its hideous visage. I supposed the vibration resounding from my gruff entreaty must have affected the life form fatally. For the palpitations abruptly ceased and it breathed no more.

"I am at a loss," said I, "Did we or did we not bare witness to a woman's pretty voice answering back?"

"We did," was the general view.

"Sack this monstrosity up and get my gardener to take it down to the potting shed for stowage. I remain unconvinced of your explanation, Arthur, but I shall, for the while, conduct my own enquiries. You may remain in my house until further notice. I am inclined to leniency, for I can see you are clearly as shocked as the rest of us concerning this queer mutation. My, dear Mr Jopson, a stiff whisky is in order."

Thus, it was that I took a leaf out of Sherlock Holmes' book, as it were, and, like him, the clever consulting detective of Baker Street, requiring a swift response, placed an advert in certain widely read periodicals, even allowing a number of notices to be pinned up around the village:

iii Wings leathery
ivi Green secretion
iiii Spasmodic twitch
Transmogriphication?
Dark forces?

Lost

I do not doubt my advertisement encouraged ridicule and scorn, amongst townsfolk and villagers alike. Boisterous good humour to flourish in local taverns. But I can report, with some warranted satisfaction, upon the twenty-seventh of January, a most enlightening occurrence took place when I was visited by a number of most distinguished individuals, including Sir George Darwin, professor of astronomy, then residing at Newnham Grange, C.W. Leyton, Downing professor of medicine, and also a physician at the university teaching Hospital — the medical sciences additionally represented by Sir Allen Seeton and Dr L. Radcliffe of the Medical College.

Sir George was quick and to the point, "Charles Darwin, my illustrious ancestor, one day at Down House, found in the garden a small, fallen meteorite. Taking scrapings, thence by diligent use of pestle and mortar, he examined this powder under a microscope and determined bacterial life existed in a preserved state of inactivity. If only one were able to reanimate, invigorate this bacterium into a live substance then inject it into a human cadaver as a host. Might it not be possible for the interplanetary life form to grow and prosper, and the original species from whatever solar system re-emerge and communicate? The specific notebook relating to this potential discovery was found by my daughter. Perfectly by chance, while on a visit after his death."

"So, you jolly clever chappies locked heads together. I believe I comprehend where this is leading. Pray, continue," said I, striking a match to my pipe.

"At the teaching hospital, I was both appalled and saddened when Amelia Lang, then suffering the latter stages of tubercular decline lay languishing in a hospital bed. A most beautiful, intelligent young woman, reduced her life shortened by this pestilent disease of the lungs and trachea — none of her own fault."

"We had been trying for ages, using cadavers as the host, without success — but Darwin's principle was still sound. The solarised bacteria remained dormant. But in living tissue might thrive," said Dr Seeton. "Incidentally, I must congratulate you on these extraordinarily fine cigars."

"My Mayfair wine merchant purchases them from Hart Melbourne & Co — Punch and Hoyo de Monterrey's — sends me boxes occasionally. More sherry anybody?" I directed my housekeeper Mrs Norton, to do the necessary — enthralled by what I had heard so far.

"You see Mr Lensby, when she became injected with solar bacterium, it did not seem that the interstellar being overly thrived, but rather Amelia herself. For within a short time, power was restored to her lungs. She seemed entirely cured of tuberculosis. She was soon out of bed radiating health and vitality. All of us naturally remained cautious and were insistent upon her confinement. Alas, who can blame her, she one night escaped, and we had not seen nor heard of the renewed young lady until your advertisement presented certain exciting possibilities. Might we see this grasshopper creation, Mr Lensby?"

Without further preamble, on the brink of some monumental scientific breakthrough, we, all of us, hurried across the garden.

Only to learn poor Jarvis my odd job man had been taken queer, suffering severe hair loss and inflammation to his face. Which he grudgingly claimed to be directly caused by the meagre remains of the interstellar being, contained in the canvas sack. An infamous residue of dust particles that, as he put it, 'glowed in the dark and radiated dangerously'.

SHROUDS UNITE

My niece Ligea Barclay was a child prodigy, at age seven she could read the complete works of Dickens, Trollope, the Brontës and Mrs Gaskell and recite passages from Swinburne and

Tennyson. By age nine, she was a gifted clairvoyant who could commune with famous dead authors and make intelligent conversation. I recall we were in deep discussion about the ghost of Irish author Sheridan Le fanu when I received a message from my housekeeper. The Reverend C.W. Warburton was apparently waiting to see me.

I hurried into the Sitting Room only to find a country parson wearing an old-fashioned, black-cocked hat, old Steinkirk tie of fine white linen, frock coat and gaiters, sitting over by the fireplace reading the Church Times.

"A rare parochial antiquity used in olden times to keep the supernatural at bay in country churchyards — interested?" he hardly bothered to look up.

"You have come about my advert." The Antiquarian assessor replied.

The cleric took a sip of port "Mr Lensby, you are an acknowledged expert on monoliths and stone circles, ancient burial rights — mine is related. An artefact, used widely by sextons in the seventeenth century, when, of course, the threat of vampires, the undead, the procession of the shrouds and other lesser churchyard phenomena such as will o' the wisps, was very real. There was, I suppose, an openness to these things, lamentably missing in this modern age of gaslight and the motor."

"You speak with some authority," I acknowledged. "But tell me, what is this fascinating antiquity — perhaps a straw head like the one in Wimbourne, Hampshire — am I on the right track?"

"No." the parson exclaimed, somewhat dismissively. "I read recently about the 'Blocksberg Tryst', an old manuscript purported to hold the key to transcendental magic. Mr Alfred Hornsby has, I believe, shown great interest in this document. I regard it and the 'straw head' with equal disdain. They are both, in my opinion, nothing more than cheap theatrical props, presented in a 'sensational' manner to dupe the public and sell newspapers."

"And yours is a genuine article?"

"Yes, it is!" replied the parson with a nod. "The instrument is fashioned from a saint's thigh bone, melded to a fragment of leaden coffin; *it is called a horror horn.*"

"May I enquire if you have brought it along with you?"

"Oh, dear me, no!" The parson answered emphatically, "But you are most welcome to a practical demonstration. My rectory is at Leaming on the east coast. You are welcome to test it under strict conditions. The Horror Horn is far from being a mere redundant antiquity kept under lock and key."

"I should be delighted. Might I bring along my niece. She is young, but interested in the unusual, keeps a journal devoted to eerie happenings. You see, my own ancient house is haunted."

"Ah, commendable, and yet in her youthful mind, is she able to fully grasp I wonder, the true horrors of a churchyard under the influence of the full moon when the dead are prone to wander and cause mischief — I put down a challenge - Next Thursday is April the thirtieth, the eve of May Day, or in Germany — Walpurgisnacht. The perfect night for an experiment. A night when witches celebrate their sabbat. Come join me if you dare."

———

We arrived at Leaming railway station at three o'clock.

A warm, sunny afternoon. Birdsong and the lazy drone of bees made our short walk to the rectory all the more enjoyable.

After lunch the Rev. C.W. Warbourton treated us to a guided tour of his rural parish. He owned a little motor which raced about the lanes most efficiently, although the brakes seemed somewhat suspect — the parson, as my niece observed, having to pump his foot at least thirty times on the pedal to get the car to stop!

That evening, we wandered about the quaint churchyard. The parson showed us various interesting, else amusing epitaphs. Although he had a troubled look about him.

"They," referring to the local coven of witches, "will be starting up soon," the parson said seriously, taking out his gold repeater and checking the time. There was a hill with a circle of trees at its summit and he surveyed this with a trained eye.

Once more he threw down the challenge "The risen moon shall soon be upon us — are you or are you not both ready and willing to engage the forces of darkness."

Frankly on that lovely April late afternoon in the sunny vicarage garden full of nesting birds, blue and great tits, the idea of wizardry or witchcraft out here in the countryside seemed far-fetched, and Ligea and myself humoured the old man, believing him to be eccentric, a bit 'over the top', intense — not exactly helpful, my niece burst into a fit of giggles, "I really must check my box camera," She spluttered, rummaging inside her shoulder bag.

"May we make a plan of the graves?" I unfolded a large sheet of paper, placing it flat against one of the tabletop tombs nearby.

"Do as you will," the parson said kindly, making the sign of the cross with a wide sweeping motion of his hand. "I have my library of religious books and tracts to consider. The mystic, Saint Joseph of Cupertino, the great thinkers, and logicians De Caspen, Valtelliana and the Dominican monk, Gorres. I must prepare for an onslaught of forces more evil than any of us dare to contemplate. We meet for supper on the half-hour! Until then, adieu!"

After our meal we retired to the study and partook of coffee.

We enjoyed the fine panorama of graves and tombs and, indeed, old Leaming church itself, seen from the study window. There was a bright full moon. The sky clear and dotted with a cluster of stars.

"What a lovely night," I remember saying, drinking my coffee.

"Such serene tranquillity abroad in a country churchyard," Ligea said gaily, tempted to quote a few lines from the poet Cowper.

"A dreadful night!" The parson spoke in direct contrast. "A night of evil – we must be on our guard."

"Why Grandpapa, there is a strange green light just appeared above one of the graves – it seems to hover there." Ligea got up and positioned herself with her little camera over by the window. The parson leapt up from his chair and tore back the curtains.

"Minor phenomena – a will o' the wisp, perhaps." He surmised, "growing larger – phosphorus texture! Some sort of ethereal substance, most likely protoplasm."

"Expanded to about the size of a party balloon, I should say," added my niece.

"No, larger still!"

The parson reached for his pince-nez. "This is no mere will o' the wisp," he murmured excitedly. "Egg-like in shape – a sort of translucent oval!"

"Yes, that's a better description," the girl agreed.

The vicar did his best to explain the phenomena.

"Now my dear, this, undoubtedly, belongs to witches' 'pharmacopoeia'. Up on the hill their sabbat will soon culminate in the Black Mass and unhallowed feats of necromancy. They have sent a diabolical agency to wrench the dead from their graves. It is much worse than I, at first, presumed. We could be about to witness the unholy procession of the shrouds."

"The procession of the shrouds..." I answered wracking my brain.

"The Horror Horn! I must retrieve it from its case! There is not much time." Abandoning his vigil, the parson rushed out of the study.

"Oh, I do so hope I can catch those pretty fluctuations of light with my camera," said Ligea, snapping away.

The green, translucent egg appeared to be exuding long writhing tentacles about the graves and tombs — searching out certain of their number on the north side. "What do you make of that, Ligea?" I asked in a school masterly way.

"Many of those would be unmarked plots," She answered primly.

"Where are buried the suicides and felons, are they not?"

"Yes, although Grandpapa they are, as you'll agree for the most part, the graves of paupers and the unbaptised — golly whizz, the egg-shaped thing is undergoing a rapid transformation — fluidic matter changing shape."

"Why, there's some sort of figure materialised with its arms outstretched — a hooded abbot! See the soil is erupting, *Thabens nomen scriptum quod nemo novit nisi ipse*, talons emerging from the turf."

The elderly parson bustled along the churchyard path and with his queer horn leapt up on to the tabletop of a large tomb.

"Begone, thou blasphemous and perverse abomination of magicians whose sorceries I shall not permit to raise ghosts in my churchyard nor the rotting undead," We heard him then shout a resounding "AMEN!"

The spectral, abbot slowly rose and turned to face the parson, seemingly encased by the protoplasmic egg. Its eerie red eyes shone all the more vividly.

"What phenomena!" I said, my nose flattened against the window.

"I will get a picture, I must, I must, I must!" Cried my niece. Click, click, click went the box camera lever.

Alas, none of her photographs ever came out.

The parson raised the Horror Horn to his lips blowing hard. There was a deep basso drone. The awesome sound filled the charged atmosphere.

In that same instant, the evil entity — with its sparkling, ethereal tentacles of light, each searching the undulating graves, reaching out to nurture a gathering of lost souls — withered and abruptly vanished.

Nunc dimittis servum tuum

All was still again, the moonlit churchyard as serene as could be, save for the chittering of bats and the odd hoot of an owl.

POOR MR COLE

One night in my study, unnoticed entirely by my erudite secretary, Mr Cole, who was assisting me by working on medieval apocrypha, was joined by what I first took to be an apparition. Neither the first, nor last, to intrude upon my fireside during long winter nights. For my old country house in Little Thornden was a haunted one.

Glancing up from translation, peering more curiously through my spectacles, I was astonished to see my friend Mr Jopson, accompanied by Mr Brunswick, materialise over by the sideboard.

They, presumably, by some magical power of the will, able to come forth. One wearing plus fours, the other a tweed suit. A latterly flickering, much fainter hologram of the pair appearing most agreeably to me in my chambers.

They both waved before vanishing altogether.

A knock came at the door some half hour later and my housekeeper Mrs Norton, presented the actual persons intact.

Thus, with a good deal of joviality, we sat down to smoke and drink fine wine. Mr Cole, quite correctly, remained in a discreet capacity absorbed by his work at my desk.

"A ceremonial within a pentagram based on the old *solve et coagula alchemical* principle. I hope one day to improve upon this by trapping molten light." proposed Mr Jopson.

"Appear and dissolve, your visual projections were commendable," I acknowledged. "Perhaps if one might extend the time ratio to say, five minutes rather than a matter of seconds."

Chatting agreeably, I went on to recount my motoring out to see that scoundrel, Old Wentworth. His practice of using for a manservant a disgusting revenant of which, by means of surgery performed in the old asylum mortuary, he had part imbibed with frugal intelligence.

Both Messrs Jopson and Brunswick were inclined to dispute, to remain sceptical preferring a 'voodoo orgy' as performed in, say, Louisiana the deep south, else the notorious island of Haiti more likely responsible for raising 'the undead' to do the bidding of its master.

At this point of the conversation Adrian Cole, my secretary, busily tasked with assisting my labours, poured scorn on our assertions.

"Really," said he, "what utter nonsense you people talk. Have I, perchance, stumbled into an Afro-Caribbean folklore society meeting — next you'll be jabbing pins into voodoo dolls."

"That's scurrilous talk. When I was your age at university, young man, I had already mastered the tenants of voodoo and, had not a friend at Trinity stopped me just in time from sticking a pin into a doll, one of our foremost liberal politicians might be dead now, long in his grave — *frater omnia viacam.*"

"*Per dum abo* — my line of reasoning. My faith, I am confident transcends any mumbo-jumbo. Your mishmash of fantastical ideas that in no way has any foundation in reality. I am Anglican and proud of it."

"Deny our certainty in centuries-old magic if you dare, Mr Cole, but your own scant beliefs, your narrow-minded attitude toward the occult questions your own sanity — not mine." Emphasised Mr Brunswick.

"Gentlemen, gentlemen, I think perhaps, Adrian, you have been argumentative enough for one night — you may leave the indexing until tomorrow — I am delighted with your work on the manuscript, by the way."

"Thank you, Mr Lensby. Goodnight gentlemen."

All of a sudden, Mr Cole turned very ashen. Undergoing an attack of panic. He jumped back, the cause, I observed, being a tiny spider. A harmless thing that scuttled across the carpet, to the skirting board. My secretary supported himself against the desk, breathing rapidly, a bubbly sheen of sweat appearing upon his brow.

"Forgive me," he gasped, "for all my life I have suffered an acute aversion – to ..."

"Arachnophobia – a fear of the common house spider," answered Mr Jopson with a knowing look. Somewhat embarrassed, Mr Cole hurried upstairs to the guestroom.

"Nice chap," I emphasised, sipping my Château d'Yquem. "At any rate, he is not afraid to speak his mind."

"No, but he lacks a real understanding of magical lore – a closed outlook," said Mr Jopson, helping himself to another Hoyo de Monterrey cigar from the box.

A warm glow infusing my vitals, due to being somewhat tight from the excellent Napoleon brandy, I could not have been more content that winter's night at my house.

Yet, the following day brought still further excitements.

It began when, surprisingly, Arthur, my grandson burst into my chambers at a quarter-past seven. Much to the chagrin of my loyal housekeeper, who protested vehemently.

The young chap had the effrontery to demand my immediate presence upstairs in the guest room.

"By jingo, I am not in the habit of being at the beck and call of my grandsons — aren't you and Tubby meant to be riding your bicycles to the agricultural college."

"There is little time Grandfather, your secretary has been taken queer. I am perhaps, understating the facts."

"What exactly do you infer?" I asked guardedly.

"Mrs Norton is frantic, please hurry!"

Once upstairs, my housekeeper did her best to explain, "You see Mr Lensby sir, a lot of banging and thumping. I goes to investigate only to find Mr Cole on the landing frothing at the mouth. But 'e went back to his room an' there was silence after — no bother, only... only... I knocked at his room this morning with a cup of tea, and 'ees on the ceiling."

What startling intelligence, we entered the guest room, astounded by what we saw.

I glanced up, my secretary was upside down. He had no body to speak of, his head supported by an arachnid's eight hairy legs grown, sprouting from the fellow's neck, secured thoroughly to the ceiling by suckers.

"Come down at once" I cried out, "breakfast is waiting."

Poor Cole only blinked. Then oozed a peculiar fluid from his mouth.

"No mind, I shall telephone Mr Jopson at once. He has been up to his tricks again. The spell shall shortly be revoked, Mr Cole. Hang on until then. Mrs Norton, be a dear and lock the door for the next twenty minutes or so, no one must be allowed to enter or leave this guest room."

The sick lamplight
shimmering on his skin

An unrelenting hypersalivation
(radiating an unnatural effervescence).

LIGEA'S DAY OUT

Overlooking the shingle beach, south of the old Battery and Martello Tower stands the lifeboat station. A sturdy timber construction that, like the stone coffin (utilised as a horse trough outside the inn), although of a more modern era, deserves notice.

I have myself looked on this further landmark occasionally from afar while enjoying my golf or taking my morning constitutional strolling the long beach. But I confess, never fully got round to visiting, nor examining, the functional building more closely.

This all changed, however, when that spring, walking along with my niece, she happened to mention, a recent coastal tragedy and this, I supposed, must have awoken my interest.

After lunching at the tearooms, we made a point of strolling up the promenade to gain a more forthright impression.

The lifeboat house, I report, was but a glorified hut. However, secured to the gleaming iron railings leading down the steps, were a forlorn number of salt-crusted, withered wreaths.

We were, Ligea and I, thus drawn to study the various memorium cards.

Each card, no doubt represented a family from Eastlea, now steeped in bereavement. Sorrow for the suddenly departed loved ones. The town's brave lifeboatmen.

"You over there," said I, recognising a local, a frequenter of the public inn, loitering about the vicinity of the lifeboat shed. "What mean this?"

I indicated to the bleak railings, the sea spray-decimated row of worn wreaths.

"Month last, sir," the rough type said, doffing his cap as is to be expected, shuffling over to join me. "A terrible big sea, a storm that had been raging along the coast all day. Eventide, a rocket goes up, a steam freighter in distress out there on the swell."

"I'd wager those poor, brave fellows responded, but never returned to this slipway due to their lifeboat severely capsizing," My niece surmised, for I knew but scant details.

"That's about the gist, young lady."

"And pray, how exactly were the, erm... "

"Bodies recovered, sir?"

I nodded.

"Well, round 'ere, the sea gives up its own, the strong current brought 'em in over the next week, some on the beach, others on the rocks."

"And naturally, as one would expect, the event being notable, a large funeral took place. The procession of many hearse and mourning coaches to yonder church with the round tower, the streets lined with those anxious to pay their last respects, as is common." Said I.

"No, it was really quiet. I don't recalls no fussy funeral cortege, as such," he sighed.

"Come man," I remonstrated, "these fellows are heroes, presumably buried up at the flint church. A permanent mortuary monument will one day be erected to record their valour... a quiet burial, you say?"

"In a grave pit on the north side. Now, I'd better be off. I have my boat to attend further along the beach. Excuse me."

"Yes, of course. Good day."

What an odd way these folk, mostly engaged in the mackerel and herring fisheries, have of showing respect for the dead, I wondered sombrely. I should have expected a decent turn out, a fine funeral procession – mourners lining the streets for the occasion. Incomers from other villages and towns. A mayor, councillors, a funeral oration delivered to a packed congregation at the flint church.

My niece and I, we decided required a deeper understanding of local custom and set off straight away for the vicarage.

The Rev J. Coryton, the rector whom I knew from previous visits to Eastlea, incredibly also appeared indifferent. Wishing to skirt around the issue, pass it off and talk of antiquarian matters.

"Well, Milton, it was last month after all, at my age can I be forgiven for the odd lapse of memory? No, on the whole, I'd recall it was a simple burial deemed for the best in the circumstances. The lifeboatmen being interred together."

"In a pit on the north side?" I queried. "You were present at the burial service, along with family members, I take it! Officials, fellow lifeboatmen?"

"Gravediggers, a sexton certainly. Now, dear boy, won't you and Ligea come in and take tea. Did you, perchance, hear Mr Laughton's recently garnered a hoard of Roman coin further inland at Westrope Hill. I must also show you a map of the standing stones. Come in, come in, let me have your hats and coats. Mr

Brunswick informs me your golf swing is improving, quite a reasonable handicap, I hear."

"Well, I suppose I must be doing something right," I chuckled, forgetful of my original intention.

"We really must arrange a day's excursion," enthused the rector. "To visit the infirmary for pauper lunatics on the outskirts of town."

"And perhaps take in St Peter's Mancroft church, the tomb of Sir Thomas Browne, author of Religio Medici. Yes, I should like that, padre," I answered contentedly. "When you're next my way, we will take a trip to the Iron Age hill fort on Thornden hill."

"Splendid, now let my housekeeper supply us with excellent hot buttered crumpets and a pot of Earl Grey. Milton, I really must catch up on all your latest news."

———

That afternoon, chatting amiably at the tea shop with Dr Plimb after an energetic if challenging round of golf due to the breezy links, Ligea an excellent putter, in fact an extremely able golfer, and very, very competitive — (she had also found time to visit the little tourist library, affiliated to The Anchor public house) we were inclined to once more broach upon the topic of the *understated* lifeboat disaster.

"I have never known such reticence Grandpapa," said Ligea Barclay. "Few fisher folk, local seamen round here, evidently seem willing to offer more than a passing nod regarding the incident. Nothing appeared in the national dailies, the local *Eastlea Messenger* for the same month carried but a brief paragraph, 'buried quickly in a grave pit on the north side'. I find that a strange state of affairs. What say you, Dr Plimb, you are, after all, the only one of us local to the community?"

"And young lady, let us not forget first to examine the drowned bodies brought ashore on the tides." Pausing to unwrap his pouch of tobacco, he made a ritual of filling his old briar. "Well., actually I've deliberately been misleading," aware of Ligea's questioning stare, he lowered his voice, looking warily about him, "Look here, I'd rather this remain hush, hush for now – discretion is of the top order. The folk of the village are united, one pointed in this affair – and tight lipped with good reason."

I ordered another round of cakes and, once our coffee cups were suitably replenished, at last I was able to be enlightened as to the truth.

"Odd, very, very odd," the doctor remarked, smoking his pipe vehemently. "The way it all started six months past. A coffin ship, the Royal Oak foundered during a terrible storm, rough seas off the eastern coast. The word 'coffin' refers to an old hulk of a vessel barely seaworthy that is deliberately scuttled, along with cargo to claim substantial insurance. We only became aware of that later, but the Eastlea lifeboat got called out, the men prepared for a tough night's work. Eventually, despite the treacherous swell, they did manage to board her, during the brief time they searched the cabins and hold for survivors, I believe, they first contracted a most singular and abhorrent contagion born of the tropics."

"So we have it at last," Ligea cried. "Quarantine is at the heart of this unwillingness on behalf of locals to elaborate."

"I regret that this was not the case."

"Were any of these ship crew of the Royal Oak ever saved?" I asked, helping myself to a fruit tartlet and passing the plate round.

"None, probably. Some abandoned the vessel earlier and taken to the long boats — but whether they survived or not remains unanswered. Anyhow, bear with me — the lifeboat returned to shore, the report being the ship, due to rotten timbers and feeble corkage, sunk fairly quickly before dawn's first light. The initial peculiarity regarding any members of the lifeboat crew, however, came to my attention when the

63

coxswain's wife, Abigail Tagg, mentioned her husband had taken to longer and longer spells of cold-water sea bathing, this in October when the shoreline can be dangerous. During the tempestuous weather of the autumn equinox, there are many demands on the Eastlea lifeboat crew, the boat launched frequently — six ships foundered — the second to last, a vessel named Providence, sailed from Boston, but one solitary survivor, a cabin boy name Tom Joye, kept afloat for a time upon a timber plank. Managing to swim ashore, he gave a revealing witness account of the wreck. Claiming, even before a sworn Justice of the Peace, that the lifeboat crew manning the craft, upon arrival and boarding, were none more than amphibian, scaly-skinned creatures with horned, shark-like heads — a great gash of a mouth filled with treble rows of barbed and rotating sharp teeth. He emphasised that they did not attempt treacherous seas to bravely rescue the crew of his ailing ship, rather to tear them to pieces and voraciously devour them. The lack of survivors from previous wrecks, I recall, had been brought into question."

"It was readily observed, even commented upon, that, returning from each perilous launch, supposedly pitting their lives against the raging elements, the lifeboatmen appeared plump and over jolly, singing bawdy sea shanties for hours, lusty with trollops. But a day or so later, the wives complained that their husbands and sons fell into a melancholy disposition, utterly losing interest in victuals, more and more inclined to sea bathing for long periods. However, there was something of greater significance that, in effect, sealed their dooms in the eyes of local fisher folk at least."

"Oh do tell us, Dr Plimb," Ligea was beside herself, desperate to know more...

"Well young lady, despite cunning attempts to conceal their affliction, although on land unable to fully transform, each member of the lifeboat crew had developed webbed, scaly hands and feet and a set of breathing organs entirely disproportionate to the face. That can only be described as gills – a deplorable indictment in itself. This, together with the truthful testimony of the cabin boy, condemned them to extinction."

"So we can take it there never was a lifeboat disaster in the first place – no men died and were later washed up. The tragedy was an invented sham." Said I.

"Precisely, Milton. The unsavoury problem was dealt with discreetly by the villagers themselves – the remains of these creatures were buried with scant ceremony, on the north side. That is all I am prepared to say on the matter — even to you young lady."

FEN END HOUSE

Always a pleasure to take a short holiday with a number of friends and make a break of it.

Well do I recall one such holiday, at the height of the summer, when Mr Jopson, Mr Brunswick, Dr Hutton and myself (all golfing cronies) travelled from Little Thornden, by way of a flying car, taking the direct route, to Cromer.

Cromer, that pleasant bathing place on the cliffs of the North Sea, as yet like certain of the other Norfolk parishes thereabouts to be overrun with sand. Else half- engulfed by the ocean.

My old Austin convertible, I'd better explain, by means of a daring magical incantation been transformed by molecular change to transcend matter, and thereby take to the air – Messrs Brunswick and Jopson were rather good at that sort of thing. Arthur,

Tubby, Ligea and Felicitina, her pet red squirrel heartily approved.

After putting up at the Sea March private hotel on the edge of the Overstrand, with fine marine views and terraced lawns leading down to the coastal path. A thoroughly respectable establishment run by a Mrs Poole, the following morning saw us cycling over to Felbrigg church, containing some notable brasses, and thence, armed with our scorecards, enjoying a bracing round of golf on the links at the Royal Cromer Club in sight of the lighthouse.

After a good lunch, a stroll upon the sandy beach was felt requisite.

It was here, by the seaside, the ocean flat and calm, the weather warm and sunny, blue

skies stretching to the far horizon, that to the east of the pavilion pier, we became alerted to a bustle of activity.

The to'ing and fro'ing of police officers close to the surf, a rowing boat having been dragged ashore.

Onlookers, loungers, and sea bathers were being encouraged to keep their distance.

Someone approaching our party of gentlemen (who I rightly surmised to be an inspector of police) had the impudence to regard us as part of the common herd.

"Move on, we want this area cleared sharpish. We can't 'ave just anybody stood about gawping, a police matter is currently in progress."

"I am not just anybody," I replied curtly, doffing my straw boater. "I am Milton Lensby an antiquarian professor and author, and incidentally, play golf with your superior, Chief Super of the County, Sir Cedric Evans. These other gentlemen are professionals also. Now explain what on earth has happened."

"Beg pardon — Inspector Thorpe," the officer replied contritely. "Well, sirs, it looks like a double suicide. Two women: one elder, the other younger. Who, according to eyewitnesses, waded out to sea and proceeded to deliberately drown 'emselves. Hard to countenance ending your life in a public place at the height of the tourist season amongst a crowd of sea bathers, but there we are. Is perchance anyone of you gents a doctor?"

"Yes, I am," replied Hutton, anxious to assist.

"Our police surgeon will later perform an autopsy, but in the meanwhile, I'd be grateful if you can give 'em a preliminary 'once over' just to confirm that two deaths have occurred — a number of fatalities."

"Lead the way, Inspector. I am a qualified medical practitioner, after all."

I confess, at this juncture, I really should have shown more restraint.

Understanding the tragic situation, left things be. Withdrawn to a more respectful distance further along the groins — two poor ladies were involved. But, alas, my curiosity got the better of me. Proved too great a pull and, like Mr Jopson and Mr Brunswick, I latched onto the doctor like a clam.

The pair had been laid out on the beach after being recovered in the rowboat and were now concealed under a tarpaulin. When the police drew back the sheets, I caught a glimpse of a fairly unattractive, plain pair.

A stern matron of more advanced years and a younger woman — both blue-lipped and waxy-faced — that spoke to me not of a violent end, nor a struggle.

Inspector Thorpe directed that the drowned bodies should be dispatched on stretchers to the waiting police van, with our assistance.

We proceeded at a sedate pace, with all dignity and respect, up the sandy beach, negotiating a set of steep granite steps to attain at last the Overstrand.

However, passing between a crowd of East Enders (worse luck who were up for the day), Cockneys gathered in flimsy sea bathing costumes to gloat unwholesomely upon the deceased, came a real shocker.

A peculiar hissing started up and we, all of us, horrified to see, despite the corpses being only minutes earlier certified dead, life extinct – started to breathe again in a loud, stertorous fashion.

Yet also remarkable, from beneath the blanket of the nearest stretcher, a scaly, webbed claw flopped limply down, the yellowish mottled talons twitching spasmodically.

Showing tact, the utmost perseverance in the line of duty, a number of stout-hearted constables, so as not to cause alarm amongst members of the public, swiftly conveyed the re-animated bodies into the rear of the police wagon. Whence doors were slammed tightly shut and bolted.

Jopson, Brunswick and myself were not to be excluded from further interesting developments, however, for aware of our credentials as witnesses, Inspector Thorpe insisted we accompany him back to Cromer police station in his Armstrong Sidley patrol car. The police wagon, meanwhile, went on ahead.

Taking place in the interview room at that most functional, blue-lamped constabulary office along Tucker Street was a transfer of data between human and an indiscernible species.

The pair being best described as 'loosely aquatic' - glutinous, bulging ovoid beings possessing multiple eyes on stalks, yet still, despite their limitations of

physiognomy, able to exude such femininity and emit properly spoken English dialect from their exposed navels. The belly button being now the vocal medium, for no mouth, as such, existed.

The women (or whatever) were far from being inhibited and proceeded to enlighten Inspector Thorpe, a dour and taciturn individual, details concerning a most bizarre circumstance.

"I am the mother-in-law, Mrs Agatha Sindrey, and this, believe or not, is my daughter Mary. Wife of that despicable cur Professor Lemsfield Specktora of Fen End House in the village of Waterbeach.

"That's five miles north-east of Cambridge." The policeman scribbled notes down onto his pad.

"If you say so, officer. Mr Specktora lost the use of his legs in a riding accident jumping fences. My husband was an invalid ... or so he claimed," spoke up the daughter.

"Whatever, Inspector, we must concern ourselves wholly with the man, the professor, the scientific beast. Who, barely married to Mary for six months, showering her with gifts and worshipping the very ground she trod, suggested quite charmingly one afternoon, whilst enjoying a sojourn along by the west bank of the River (of which his manor house overlooked) that we, the mother-in-law and the wife, might care to both be first to benefit from an exciting new health and beauty development he was pioneering. By which ladies might become younger, vivacious, and more glamorous to behold in an entirely natural, uncomplicated way. Free of exercise regimes and finicky diets, and lotions and potions. He proposed a series of injections to which both I and my daughter agreed. We received our dosages of serum three times daily without complaint, in a spirit of perfect equanimity, awaiting keenly the promised results in the reflection of the looking glass."

"A woman's vanity must be upheld — yes, I'm entirely clear on that point. Please continue, Mrs Sindrey," said the inspector sombrely, his clean- shaven face both graven and serious.

At this juncture in proceedings, the poor ladies relapsed into more stertorous breathing, worse still, additionally, it appeared the oily skin consistency beholden to both varicoloured bloated forms was becoming unstable, quivering like undulating jelly free from the mould.

"Pardon me, but when did you decide to take your own lives, to commit suicide?" The inspector was anxious to move the questioning along. "You presumably came down by train, already determined on your penultimate actions."

"But there you are mistaken, Inspector. It never was suicide in the first place. It was the only course left open to us — when we were dragged out of the sea, both of us were on the brink of change. Our heart rate and electric brain waves brought down to a minimum. Our pulses would have hardly registered for the process of becoming cold-blooded had begun and had we been left alone; we should have quite naturally swum out to deep water. Allowed at least to survive."

Alas, I can only report the end was approaching. No administrations, no attempts by Dr Hutton to save the lives of the pair could hope to succeed. For the personage of Agatha Sindrey and Mary Specktora, of whatever alien persuasion, began a rapid meltdown. Lasting a further ten minutes duration until only two slimy puddles of an obscure green effluent remained, adhering to the linoleum floor beneath the interview desk.

Due to these unparalleled circumstances, not viable to debate in a court of law, else repeatable before a sane judge and jury, the police at Cromer were reluctant to pursue the matter further and showed little inclination to press charges.

We, on the other hand, that is Hutton, Mr Jopson, Mr Brunswick and myself. The golfing crowd. Were determined to learn more, to go to East Anglia and visit Fen End House.

Thus, abandoning our golfing holiday, we paid up our hotel bill, bid Mrs Poole a fond adieu and lost no time.

Motoring across country, Norfolk to Suffolk, Suffolk into Cambridgeshire. Mr Jopson, gripping the wheel with his foot down hard, testing my Austin convertible's combustion engine to its very limits, latterly took us through Bury St Edmunds. Charging across, part flying over the county to Newmarket, until

we encountered amongst the interminable flatlands, those arable open field stripes. Penetrated by the artificial drains of Waterbeach level — the village standing within the southern tip of the parish close to a river.

Accelerating past long crofts and rows of agricultural cottages, we took the back lane called Fen Road, east of the village green, where were a group of shops and houses.

Soon enough, the professor's property was in our sights.

Fen End House was a seventeenth-century half-timbered manor, set back from the river with mullioned windows and two gabled storeys of differing patterns. The steeply pitched, clay tiled roof adorned by immense twists of herringbone brick chimneys, stretching up into the evening sky.

Having made splendid time, the Austin was parked beside a verge. A sign boarded timber style, set between banked-up hedgerow trees indicated a footpath leading along the riverbank.
We got out to take in the view of the house.

"Toad of Toad Hall — so we meet at long last," quipped Mr Brunswick, stuffing his pipe full of tobacco from a shared pouch. It was still yet light, the sun shone.

"Your levity is premature," I warned. "The professor could turn out to be very dangerous."

"You see, Milton," said Dr Hutton wryly, "suppose we pretend we're a lot of jolly birdwatchers lost our way, ambled off the beaten track — he may even invite us in for a cup of tea."

"Not for an injection, I trust," said I, meaning every word. "I would be rather cagey regarding hospitality. Room and board for the night I should politely decline. I would like to examine those outhouses, the reed-thatched barn near the main habitation once it gets dark. We can put up at an inn. I'd like to wash and dine. Back in the car I saw a suitable alehouse on the green advertising accommodation."

Grateful to stretch our legs after the long journey prior to paying a cursory visit to see whether the professor was at home, we decided on a stroll along the banks of the river.

Fairly deep and wide at this point with a number of steam launches and leisure craft in evidence, it was a glorious evening.

Up above the terraces, Fen End House – was a most venerable and pleasing residence. A golden sunset enhancing the well-weathered oak, the rusty-red brickwork.

I was considering, thus, the fine architecture when Mr Brunswick tapped me on the shoulder.

Pointing his stout ash stick at the reeds drew my attention to a greenish, pulpy mush adhering to the sloping bank – a detached scaly-skinned claw lying in the mud a little further on.

"Could this be yet another result of that scientifically formulated serum? Are we, gazing at a similar monstrosity to the mother-in-law, or at least its remains?" Put forward Dr Hutton. Even as a medico, at a loss to identify the body type.

"Quite similar," I agreed.

Up until this slimy discovery, I was perhaps more concerned with seeking out a good dinner and bottle of wine, but now my curiosity reawakened. I knew it was imperative we make haste to Fen End House and confront the professor. Try to seek out answers and find out what in heaven's name was at the root of his foul experimentation.

By way of a small iron gate leading under a rose arbour and climbing terraced steps, I and the others were able to get round the side of the house and attain the front porch.

There was no bell pull, nor door knocker of any description. So, with no other option, I was about to rap hard with my knuckles when keenly wise intuition decided me towards a more cautious approach.

Leaning my ear to the nail-studded oak door, listening intently I was made aware of a peculiar slushing sound.

Mr Jopson's prising open of the letter box quietly drew our attention to the retreating bulk of a jelly-like organism that answered the summons issued from a distant room on the ground floor.

A dull, surly croaking occurred.

"Phyllis, Miss Layne," an irritated voice called out along the hall. "For goodness' sake, come in here and remove the tray. Are you going to take forever? You did not do a very good job of dusting the mantelpiece and the carpet in my study need sweeping, and I want that skirting board cleaned with a damp cloth. It's nearly time for your injection and once it's dark, we can go for a swim together. Although I must say, you don't deserve it! I expect better from a maid in my employ."

Another dull croaking response, a slithering across parquet flooring.

Dr Hutton had a brilliant idea. Suggesting, in whispered conspiratorial tones that we go round to the rear of the house and peer in at the French windows perhaps. We might catch a glimpse of our scientist, the master of the household. Or the below-stairs sub-species who were at his every beck and call.

Peering collectively in at the French windows without discovery, nobody about in the garden. Servants presumably being busy indoors, we were in luck.

For whom did we spy unawares, but Lemsfield Specktora himself.

A pleasant looking, middle-aged fellow, salt and pepper hair, a neatly trimmed waxed moustache, comfortably wearing a dressing gown. Sat before the hearth in a kind of high-winged armchair, a customised wheeled contraption. Puffing on his briar pipe reading the Daily Telegraph.

That was the head and torso, the top half of him.

Below the waist, however, was an entirely different matter. For, incongruous to human anatomy, no limbs existed in the proper sense. Rather writhing tentacles submerged under a pinky, bubbling solution.

Contained in what may be described (for simplicity's sake) as a large, waist-high fish tank, the base bolted onto where the footrest should be.

"So that's it," whispered Hutton, being a medical man able to explain. "In order that sexual congress may take place... let us speculate, that this alien being, perhaps to perform in the normal way - the originally from the oceans of Mars, clearly unable professor's nether regions resembling those of a squid - thus seeks

to adjust the female form to best suit his own species."

"To procreate. So that his own kin may thrive," I expostulated. "Yes, I catch your drift. I will write a formal letter of invitation for Professor Specktora to visit our science faculty at the university – they need to observe him more closely over a long period. Every courtesy must be forthcoming."

"But what of the innate dangers of his kind?" questioned Mr Jopson doubtfully as we hurried back to the car "Particularly to women!"

"He must be scientifically analysed for the greater protection of mankind," I replied curtly.

The following morning, well rested after a hearty breakfast of ham and eggs. Provided with half pints of warm beer by the friendly landlord at the Windy Miller alms-house on the green, the general view was that before motoring off in my convertible to the Gog Magog hills for a round of golf, we should pay a visit to close-by Fen Church. For which my Bradshaw's guide was most complimentary. Noting first-rate brasses, one silver-gilt chalice from 1552, a finely embossed cup made in 1557 presented by Marjory, wife of Thomas Banks, resembling in shape a tazza of Venetian glass.

Inlaid behind the altar were figures of saints in mosaic and similar mosaic panels by Powell of Whitefriars.

So, the old church was well worth exploring.

A short walk across the village green, surrounded by the fire engine house, residences and shops dotted about, brought us to a small churchyard.

I felt surely inadequate for so populous a parish. The thirteenth-century church building itself was constructed chiefly of field stones dressed in ashlar. Including the lower part of the west bell tower, the upper spire, I surmised, blown down in a fierce gale and later restored.

Approaching the porch, we were encouraged by a solitary jam jar left along the stone seat for visitor donations. Together with a sheaf of local history pamphlets.

One of the oak planked entrance doors to the church stood ajar, thus, after depositing our coin, we entered the cool of the place.

Struck by the tidy, well-polished interior.

Of antiquarian interest, an old, plain, square wooden pulpit and a window with perpendicular tracery displaying the manorial arms of Burgoyne and Cutts.

While we trod purposefully up the aisle to view the mosaic altar panels, the rows of pews either side I judged to be the original oak installations and not later Victorian pinewood replacements, Mr Jopson wandered over to a side door situated in a bay off the nave.

A handwritten notice pinned to the door proclaiming:

Crypt Flooded

No Entry!

For myself, I hardly cared less, more eager to attain the choir stalls and examine the mosaics. I was therefore surprised when I heard the poor fellow being violently sick. The profuse fit of vomiting was enhanced by a series of echoes, caused by the stout walls and buttresses supporting the late medieval lean-to roof above.

Voices rang out and in no time we, ourselves, had reached the entrance to the crypt. The door wide open to find our companion bent over double at the top of the steps retching.

It was not hard to determine why!

Down in the depths, the crypt floor was awash with stagnant water. Escaped possibly from a damaged conduit pipe leading from the river, part of the extensive land drainage system adopted hereabouts.

Pressure of incoming water at a higher level than was now evident, had freed the lids from corrupt coffins, so that remains of the dead now shared space with something else.

Slopping about were part-submerged living organisms... a keening monstrous herd of giant glistening pupae. Wriggling and writhing about in one green pulsating mass.

The only sensible conclusion to be had was that here in this charnel breeding ground, existed the multitudinous, repulsive progeny of Professor Specktora.

"What can be done? What can be done Milton?" gasped Mr Brunswick, seizing my arm for support. "This is worse than the worst nightmare. I mean rats are capable of breeding at an alarming rate, what if ...?"

"Y'know I enjoy a pipe as well as the next man," said I, not allowing myself to give way to hysterics. "And I always make sure I have a box of matches handy to light it with — do you follow? We are not without a means of destroying these things."

The chaps soon twigged what I was hinting at.

Grabbing any dry kindling to hand, old curtaining

and - I am ashamed to admit - early English hymnals and prayer books, we set about creating flaming torches.

Lighter fluid played its part and, bracing ourselves against the foetid atmosphere, we went down into the crypt.

Knee deep in floodwater, assaulted by the loathsome stench, we proceeded to jab and poke at the repulsive pupae, satisfied the vulnerable blubber should quickly destruct — and this proved to be the case.

This task (however unpleasant) completed; we gathered once more outside the church porch to congratulate one another on a job well done.

A return to the Windy Miller in order for a change of clothes and a round or two of drinks to celebrate — yet an emergency bell, the ringing of the village fire engine alerted us to still more destructive potency in the vicinity.

Fen End House was brightly ablaze. The whole structure an inferno. The roof caving in, smoke billowing up into the sky.

The vicar, a delightful fellow by the name of Digwyn (thank goodness a man of the cloth), not an alien intruder, offered the latest news.

"Dear me, gentlemen," he sighed, his voice full of pathos. "One hoped, one prayed that the professor

and his devoted staff escaped immolation, yet I am
mortified to report so far not one survivor has yet been
sighted. Alas, we must fear the worst. The manor is in
ruins and the worthy folk inhabiting it are no more. Two
further pumps were in attendance, one fire appliance
from Longstanton, the other Oakington. God rest their
souls."

Illustrated by Karl Whiteley

Clever Mr. Beaver

*Clever Mr. Beaver & Mr Toad's
Garden Railway Mystery*

*Clever Mr Beaver and the Baby Dragon Who Ran
Out of Puff*

———

Illustrated by Sharon Maynard Burrows

Fairytale Detective

Halloweenland

Betty's Chronicles of Glim Glumswick

———